TEEN CHALLENGES

PUBERTY

by Marcia Amidon Lusted

CONTENT CONSULTANT

Cynthia Corbitt, PhD
Associate Professor, Biology Department
University of Louisville

Essential Library

An Imprint of Abdo Publishing | abdobooks.com

ABDOBOOKS.COM

Published by Abdo Publishing, a division of ABDO, PO Box 398166, Minneapolis, Minnesota 55439. Copyright © 2022 by Abdo Consulting Group, Inc. International copyrights reserved in all countries. No part of this book may be reproduced in any form without written permission from the publisher. Essential Library™ is a trademark and logo of Abdo Publishing.

Printed in the United States of America, North Mankato, Minnesota.
102021
012022

Cover Photos: Ranta Images/iStockphoto, foreground; iStockphoto, background
Interior Photos: Creativa Images/Shutterstock Images, 4; iStockphoto, 6, 15, 26, 51, 76–77; SDI Productions/iStockphoto, 8, 12; Ali Kocakaya/iStockphoto, 16 (top), 16 (bottom); Andrew Syred/Science Source, 19; Dragon Images/iStockphoto, 22; Shutterstock Images, 28, 32, 54–55, 66–67; Quality Stock Arts/Shutterstock Images, 36–37; New Africa/Shutterstock Images, 39; Oleg Golovnev/Shutterstock Images, 42; Mike Shots/Shutterstock Images, 46–47; Dragon Images/ Shutterstock Images, 48; Motortion Films/Shutterstock Images, 56; Monkey Business Images/Shutterstock Images, 60, 80; Daniel Jedzura/Shutterstock Images, 64; David Tonelson/Shutterstock Images, 69; Karel Noppe/Shutterstock Images, 70; Fat Camera/iStockphoto, 72; LightField Studios/Shutterstock Images, 84; Monkey Business Images/iStockphoto, 89; Daisy Daisy/Shutterstock Images, 91; Leo Patrizi/iStockphoto, 92; Oleksandra Bolotina/Shutterstock Images, 95; Michael Jung/Shutterstock Images, 99

Editor: Megan Ellis
Series Designer: Colleen McLaren

LIBRARY OF CONGRESS CONTROL NUMBER: 2021941233

PUBLISHER'S CATALOGING-IN-PUBLICATION DATA

Names: Lusted, Marcia Amidon, author.

Title: Puberty / by Marcia Amidon Lusted

Description: Minneapolis, Minnesota : Abdo Publishing, 2022 | Series: Teen challenges | Includes online resources and index.

Identifiers: ISBN 9781532196287 (lib. bdg.) | ISBN 9781098218096 (ebook)

Subjects: LCSH: Puberty--Juvenile literature. | Teenagers--Physiology--Juvenile literature. | Adolescent psychology--Juvenile literature. | Adolescence-- Juvenile literature. | Teenagers--Development--Juvenile literature.

Classification: DDC 612.661--dc23

CONTENTS

Puberty can be a confusing time for teens, especially for those who may not be prepared for the changes in their bodies.

CHAPTER ONE

WHAT'S GOING ON?

Katy ducks into the restroom in the science building with only minutes to spare before her chemistry class. When she pulls down her pants in the stall, she can't stop herself from letting out a gasp. Her underwear and the inside of her jeans are stained with what looks like old, brown blood.

She tries not to panic. Katy knows about periods and the menstrual cycle from her seventh-grade health class, but that hadn't prepared her to get her first period in the middle of a school day. It also hadn't prepared her for just how much blood there could be. Quickly she stuffs some toilet paper into her underwear, pulls her jeans up, takes off her sweatshirt, and ties it around her waist. Her stomach hurts. The bell

> "I DEVELOPED REALLY EARLY. I HAD BOOBS AT NINE. I GOT MY PERIOD AT 11. SO, MY BODY WAS GOING FASTER THAN MY BRAIN. IT'S FUNNY, BECAUSE WHEN YOU'RE A LITTLE KID, YOU DON'T THINK OF YOUR BODY AT ALL. AND ALL OF A SUDDEN, YOU LOOK DOWN AND YOU'RE, LIKE, WHOA."[1]
>
> *—BILLIE EILISH, SINGER*

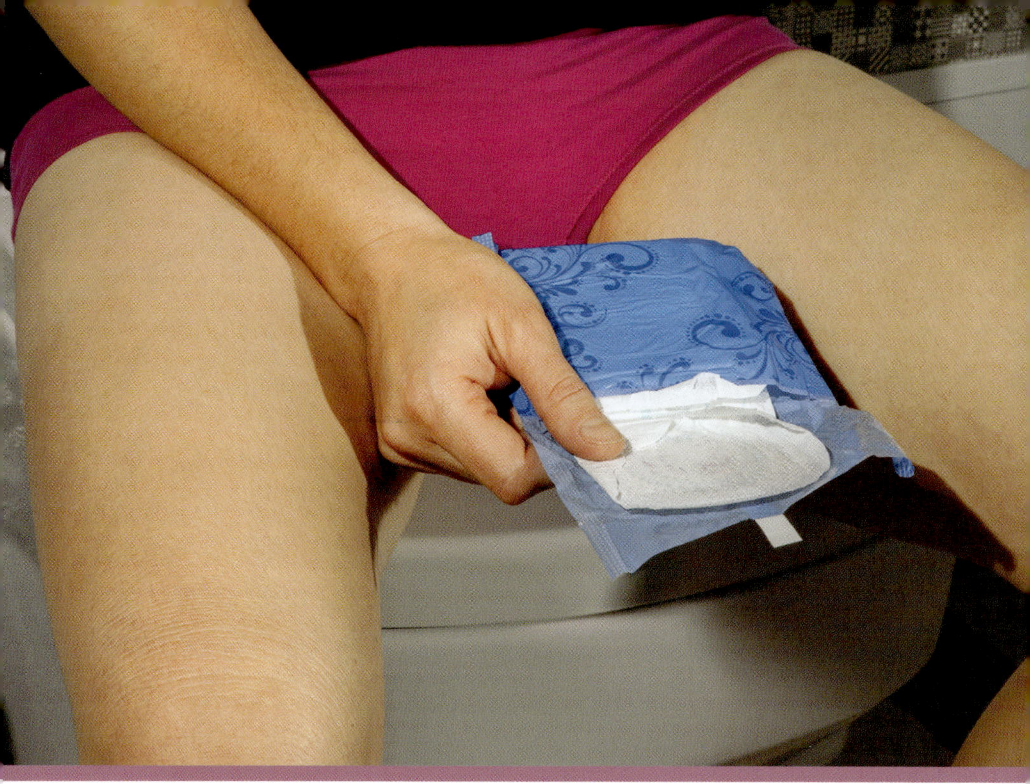

Menstrual pads have adhesive tape on the back. This helps them stick to the fabric of a pair of underwear.

signaling the beginning of class rings in the hallway, and Katy feels very overwhelmed.

Katy goes to the nurse's office, almost in tears. The nurse is sympathetic and comforting when Katy nervously knocks on the door. "Let's get you some clean clothes," she says, pulling out a pair of sweatpants and some underwear from a cupboard. "I have some menstrual pads here too." The nurse explains how to attach a pad to clean underwear, and Katy takes the items to the bathroom in the nurse's office. Her stomach is still clenched with nerves, but Katy breathes a sigh of relief when she opens the pad and it seems easy enough to stick to the underwear.

Katy's experience with her first period is very common. She had started to develop breasts two years ago, so her menstrual cycle was right on schedule. But she only knew a little bit about the process and how to take care of herself, and she was caught by surprise, as many girls are. When she got home that afternoon, she told her mom what had happened, and her mom provided her with all the supplies she needed. From then on, Katy always carried menstrual supplies in her backpack, just in case.

IS IT A PERIOD?

The first menstrual period can be confusing, especially because the person may or may not know whether it is actually a period. Every person has a different first period. There might be a great deal of blood, or there might be very little. It might be bright red in color or brownish. How often a period occurs and how long it lasts can be irregular for the first few years of menstruation. It can also be affected by things such as nutrition, sports, and medications.

PATRICK'S STORY

Patrick looks down at his pile of clothes on the bench in the boys' locker room. His towel is wrapped snugly around his entire body. In the locker room, everyone rinses off in open showers with no walls and no privacy. Patrick dreads this every day because he hates to take off his shirt in front of other people. Patrick feels like all the other boys in the

It can be easy for teens to compare themselves and their looks to others in locker rooms and bathrooms.

locker room have clear skin on their faces and bodies, and he feels extremely self-conscious about the acne spreading over his shoulders and down his back.

Patrick wishes it was like when he was younger, when he didn't have any acne at all. He didn't even think twice about taking off his shirt for gym, swimming, or playing basketball at the park on a hot day. Gym had always been one of his favorite classes, but now he hates it because he knows he'll have to face mean comments from the other boys every day.

Patrick takes a deep breath and drops his towel, grabbing his clothes to change as quickly as possible so other people don't see him. Later this week he has an appointment with a dermatologist to talk about medications that might help control his acne. But for now, Patrick thinks about how his dad told him to shift his perspective. Patrick's acne may make him feel self-conscious, but his growing muscles have really come in handy on the basketball team.

NEW EXPERIENCES

Both Katy and Patrick are experiencing different stages of puberty. Puberty is the time when the body transitions from childhood to adulthood. The word comes from the Latin word *puber*, which means "adult." Once a person goes through puberty, he or she is generally able to reproduce.

COMPARISONS

It's common for boys to compare themselves to other boys. This is especially true in locker-room situations, given that middle school and high school boys can vary so much in their development. Some boys might already be starting to develop broad shoulders and larger, stronger muscles. Others will still be thin and small.

Some boys might be tempted to start lifting weights in order to build muscle and catch up to other boys who are further along into puberty. However, before puberty really starts, weight lifting can only tone the muscles that are already there, not build them up in size. Some doctors recommend that boys wait to start weight lifting until after they've begun puberty. That way, they don't accidentally injure their growing muscles and bones.

During puberty, the body undergoes the last rapid, significant growth of a person's lifetime. The brain goes through changes too. Emotions can be stronger, and people may be much more sensitive than usual or more prone to anger. All of these are normal results of the brain making the transition from childhood to adulthood.

It can feel like everything is suddenly confusing and out of control, and there are many other emotions, both exciting and frightening, in the mix. However, these changes ultimately make people into more mature human beings, both physically and emotionally. Sara Johnson, an assistant professor at the Johns Hopkins Bloomberg School of Public Health, explains this change:

> *It is the first time [that teens] are seeing themselves in the world, meaning their greater autonomy has opened their eyes to what lies beyond their families and schools. They are asking themselves for perhaps the first time: What kind of person do I want to be and what type of place do I want the world to be?*[2]

Unlike some of the other challenges that tweens and teens face, such as family conflicts, bullying, drug and alcohol abuse, and anxiety over academics or relationships, puberty happens to everyone. However, it doesn't happen to any two people in exactly the same way or on the same timeline. Every person's body is different, just as experiences with puberty are different.

Puberty is a shared experience and a gateway to the future. It may bring about confusion, fear, and embarrassment, but it takes place at a time when a teen is typically surrounded by other teens who are experiencing the same thing. Ultimately, it brings many great things and carries the excitement of entering the adult world, with all its experiences, opportunities, and responsibilities. Knowing what to expect and being as prepared as possible for what is coming can help teens face the challenges of puberty.

AM I NORMAL?

Teens might wonder whether their bodies are normal as they go through puberty. But the truth is that there is no one "normal" body because no two people are alike. Characteristics such as hair color, eye color, body type, and height are determined by genetics. Similarly, teens may find they have very different breast sizes than their friends or different experiences with acne or muscle growth. Instead of worrying about whether they are normal, teens should work to make sure their bodies and minds are healthy.

Anatomical models can help students understand parts of the human body, including the reproductive and endocrine systems.

CHAPTER TWO

REPRODUCTIVE AND ENDOCRINE SYSTEMS

Many preteens hear the word *puberty* before the process begins in their own bodies, but they may not be familiar with what puberty entails or how it works. Puberty is the process through which teens reach sexual maturity and gain the ability to reproduce. The changes that happen during puberty begin in the reproductive and endocrine systems inside the body.

Each person's reproductive system includes external and internal organs, including gonads, which are human ovaries and testicles. Gonads are glands that create reproductive hormones and sex cells. These sex cells are eggs, which are created in the ovaries, and sperm, which are created in the testicles. Testicles and ovaries release hormones that regulate a person's reproductive system. People's reproductive systems can look and function differently whether they have ovaries or testicles.

THE VULVA AND INTERNAL GENITAL ORGANS

The vulva is an external genital organ in the female reproductive system that contains the mons pubis, the labia, and the clitoris. The mons pubis is a pad of fatty tissue that covers the pubic bone. During puberty, it becomes covered with hair. It also has glands that produce pheromones, which affect sexual attraction. Labia are folds of tissue that enclose and protect other external genital organs as well as the opening to the vagina and urethra. The clitoris is a small organ near the top of the vulva that produces sexual pleasure when stimulated. These external organs protect the internal genital organs from germs, provide sexual pleasure, and enable sperm to potentially fertilize an egg.

THE BARTHOLIN GLANDS

Bartholin glands are located next to the vaginal opening. They secrete a thick fluid that provides lubrication for sexual intercourse. Sometimes bacteria and other debris block the opening to these glands, which causes fluid to build up. This creates an abscess of pus and swollen tissue, also known as a cyst. Most Bartholin gland cysts go away on their own with at-home remedies. However, if these cysts cause symptoms such as a fever or pain while walking or sitting, they may need antibiotics or other treatments from a health-care provider.

The uterus, *center*, starts small, but it can expand during the course of a pregnancy to accommodate a growing fetus.

The internal genitals in the female reproductive system exist for sexual pleasure as well as for creating a pregnancy. These organs consist of the vagina, uterus, ovaries, and fallopian tubes. The ovaries release eggs that travel through the fallopian tubes to the uterus. When sperm enters through the vagina, it can combine with an egg to fertilize it. There is also a membrane called the hymen, which encircles or covers the vaginal opening. The hymen can tear or break during sexual intercourse, as well as through other strenuous activities such as riding horses or playing contact sports.

THE FEMALE REPRODUCTIVE SYSTEM

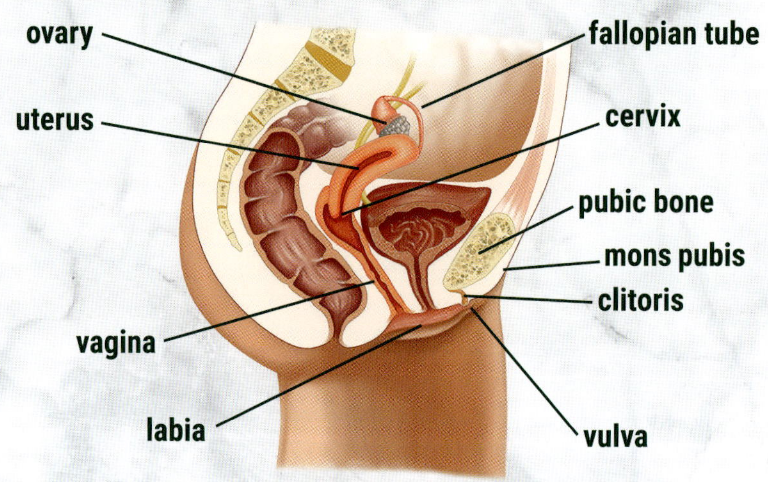

THE MALE REPRODUCTIVE SYSTEM

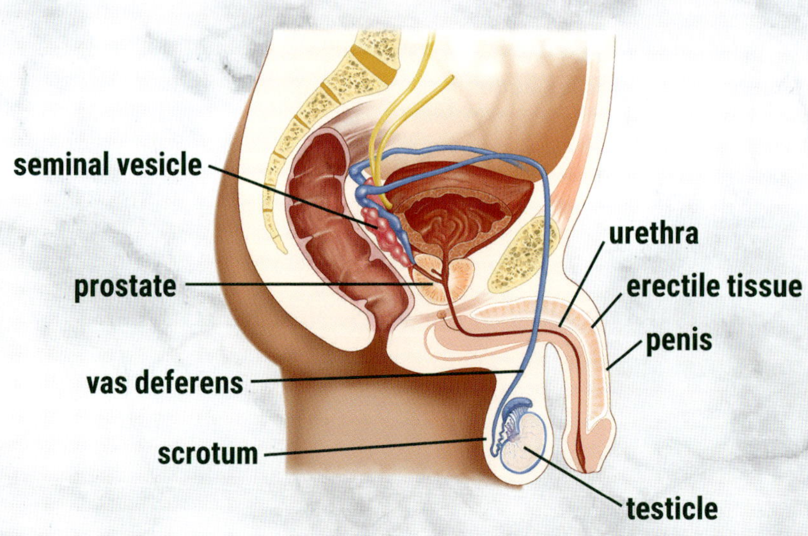

Reproductive systems include both internal and external organs.

The ovaries produce eggs and hormones, such as estrogen and progesterone, that are necessary for reproduction. The ovaries contain more than one million eggs at birth. Typically, the ovaries release one egg per menstrual cycle. During all the years of menstruation and active reproduction, however, the ovaries only release approximately 400 eggs.[1] Most eggs stay dormant, and they can be damaged with age. By the time menopause starts, most of the eggs have either deteriorated and been reabsorbed into the body or been cast off during menstruation. This continues until all of them are gone.

THE PENIS AND INTERNAL GENITAL ORGANS

The penis, scrotum, and testicles are external genital organs in the male reproductive system. The penis is part of two systems: the reproductive system and the urinary system.

RAGING HORMONES

Some people use the term *raging hormones* to explain the mood swings, stress, and sexual feelings that teens experience during puberty. The actual hormone responsible for these changes was not identified until 2007. The body releases this hormone, THP, in response to stress. In adults, THP has a calming effect and can help reduce stress. But during puberty, this hormone increases anxiety.[2] This discovery about THP in teens may help scientists deal with some of the more extreme emotional difficulties that those undergoing puberty experience.

This means that unlike the vaginal canal, which is not involved in urination, the penis allows both urine and semen to leave the body. This happens through the urethra. Inside the penis are three cylinder-shaped spaces containing erectile tissue. This tissue fills with blood during arousal to make the penis erect. The scrotum is a thick sac of skin that holds the testicles, also called the testes. In order to function properly, testicles need to be slightly cooler than a person's body temperature. The scrotum keeps the testicles safe and cool, hanging slightly apart from the rest of the body. Testicles have two jobs: to produce sperm and to produce the hormone testosterone.

INTERSEX PEOPLE

According to the Intersex Society of North America, someone who is intersex has one of a "variety of conditions in which a person is born with a reproductive or sexual anatomy that doesn't seem to fit the typical definitions of female or male."[3] For example, some intersex people may have an external penis and scrotum combined with internal ovaries and a uterus. Or, they may have external genitalia that appear different from those of others. Additionally, some intersex people do not have any obvious physical differences.

Conversations about puberty and reproductive health often leave out intersex people, even though intersex people make up an estimated 1 to 2 percent of people born in the United States. "We are here," says Johnny, an intersex interviewee in *Teen Vogue*. "Our bodies are not wrong. Our bodies break the binary. Our bodies are whole."[4]

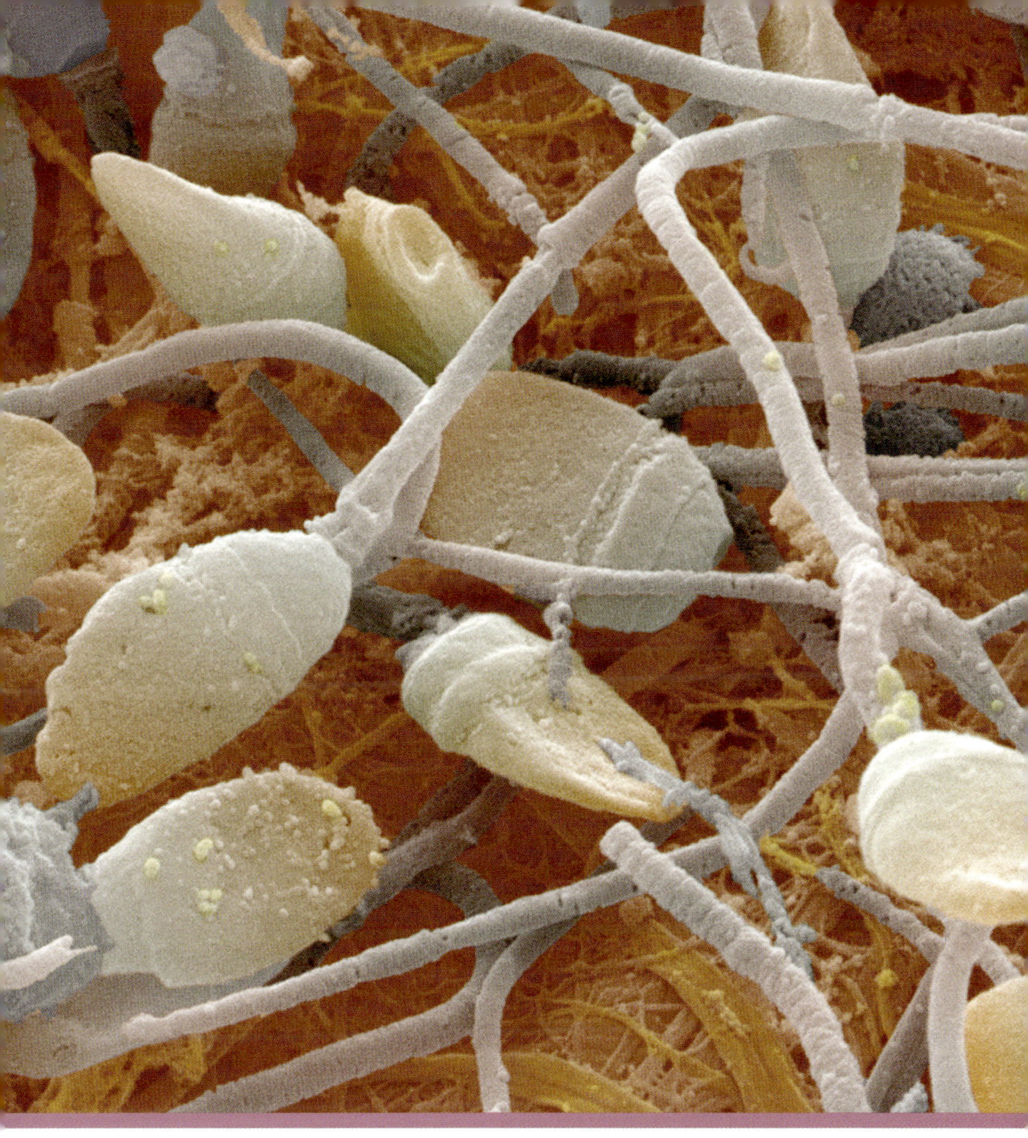

A sperm cell, such as one of the above, enters an egg cell to fertilize it. Each egg is fertilized by only one sperm.

Internal genital organs in the male reproductive system include the vas deferens, prostate, and seminal vesicles. The vans deferens is a tube the size of a strand of spaghetti that carries the sperm from the testicles to the prostate and the seminal vesicles. Sperm is then ejaculated from the penis during sexual intercourse.

HORMONAL CHANGES

The reproductive systems are responsible for most of the changes that begin happening with the onset of puberty. The changes are not just limited to the reproductive system and will include growth in other parts of the body as well. These changes happen because of specific messengers that signal the body to start the process of sexual maturation: hormones.

Hormones aren't just important for puberty and sexual maturation. There are hormones circulating through the human body that coordinate processes for growth and metabolism too. Hormones are produced and stored by different glands, which make up the body's endocrine system.

During puberty, the brain sends a signal to the pituitary gland, which responds by secreting hormones. These hormones are transported to the gonads through the bloodstream. In turn, the gonads secrete hormones such as testosterone and estrogen into the blood. Other hormones, such as androgens, are created in the adrenal glands. Androgens control hair growth during puberty, among other things.

Before a person is even born, hormones guide the development of the brain and reproductive system. They can affect how the immune system works in humans, as well as how the body uses food and turns it into energy. Hormones are the body's way of communicating with itself when important events are taking place in the body's systems.

THE ENDOCRINE SYSTEM

The hormones in the endocrine system regulate the body's metabolism, growth and development, sexual function and reproduction, sleep, and mood. The endocrine system consists of the pituitary gland, thyroid gland, parathyroid glands, adrenal glands, pancreas, and gonads, among others. The thyroid gland serves as a master metabolic control center for the body's functions, including body temperature; the function of the brain, heart, and kidneys; growth; and the function of the muscles.

Each gland removes materials from the blood, processes those materials, and then secretes a finished chemical product to be used in various parts of the body. The endocrine system acts like a messaging system throughout the body. Hormones travel through the body to glands and organs. Cells that have hormone receptors can receive these hormones and act on the message.

The stages of puberty occur over the course of many years between childhood and late adolescence.

CHAPTER THREE

AGES AND STAGES

Between 1949 and 1971, pediatrician James M. Tanner conducted a long-term study of how children grow. Tanner studied the same children over a number of years as they developed from children into teens. In 1969, he created the Tanner scale to measure physical development and the stages of puberty.[1] The Tanner scale can be useful for helping young people know what to expect as they begin puberty.

TANNER STAGE ONE

The first Tanner stage describes bodies before puberty begins. Toward the end of this stage, the brain begins to send messages to the rest of the body in order to begin puberty. These messages are specific hormones that are responsible for the changes of puberty.

Changes begin in a small part of the brain called the hypothalamus. The hypothalamus is responsible for some major body functions, such as regulating body temperature, appetite, and emotional responses; managing sexual behavior; and releasing hormones. Gonadotropin-releasing hormone (GnRH) activates at the end of stage one. It travels to the pituitary gland, which is located at the base of the brain.

The pituitary gland secretes hormones into the bloodstream, including luteinizing hormone (LH) and follicle-stimulating hormone (FSH), in response to GnRH. LH regulates the function of the ovaries and testes, and it causes the production of sex hormones. FSH is responsible for the growth of ovarian follicles, which produce the hormones estrogen and progesterone and help maintain the menstrual cycle in girls. FSH also helps to produce sperm in boys. These first signals of puberty usually start

PUBERTY AND SOCIOECONOMIC STATUS

Socioeconomic status (SES) is the measure of a person's or group's position in a society. For example, someone from a wealthy background who received a college education has a higher SES than someone from a poor background who did not go to college. Some factors that contribute to a person's SES include race, gender, education, and occupation.

Puberty occurs on a slightly different timeline for people of different SESs. While researchers aren't exactly sure why this occurs, it seems to be related to factors such as birth weight, how healthy the developing baby was inside the womb, and weight gain through the first eight years of life.[2] These factors can occur as a result of different access to health care, nutritious foods, and education for people among different SESs.

between ages eight and ten, but they don't cause any
noticeable changes in children's bodies at this stage.

TANNER STAGE TWO

With the beginning of the second Tanner stage, the body
begins to show some of the physical changes brought on
by the hormonal messengers. This stage usually begins
between ages nine and 11. One of the noticeable changes
is the growth of the
breast tissue in girls.
Breast buds appear
first. These are small,
nickel-sized bumps under
the nipples. Growth may
not be the same from one
breast to the other, so one
side might start growing
before the other side and
be larger, which is normal.
Breasts usually catch up to each other in size with time.
The buds may also be itchy or sore, which is also normal
and eventually stops. Additionally, the areolae, the colored
areas surrounding the nipples, start to expand.

During stage two, the scrotum and testicles also grow.
As the testicles grow, the skin of the scrotum changes,
becoming thinner, darker in color, and covered with tiny

As breasts grow, they may be painful or uncomfortable.

hair follicles. The scrotum will also start to hang down farther away from the body. It is common for one testicle to hang lower than the other.

Pubic hair growth also begins in this stage. This hair grows on the mons pubis or at the base of the scrotum. It might be slightly curly, but it is not yet the stiff, wiry pubic hair of adults.

Most adolescents gain weight and experience increased appetite during puberty. Some of this is to prepare menstruating bodies for their first periods. Fat often settles around the stomach during this time. During later growth stages, the body redistributes fat to the breasts and hips as a girl grows taller.

TANNER STAGE THREE

The third Tanner stage marks the point where the physical changes of puberty become more obvious. The breast buds continue to grow and expand, although the nipples are still flat on the breast and do not stick up. Pubic hair will start to get thicker and curlier, and hair may also start to grow in the armpits. For some, armpit and pubic hair may start to grow well before the breast buds are noticeable. Girls will start to build fat on their hips and thighs, and in some cases, their waists may narrow.

For boys, the penis and testicles also grow, and muscles get larger. The larynx, or voice box, and vocal cords also enlarge. This causes a person's voice to drop from a higher to a lower pitch. A person's voice may even crack when trying to speak, but the cracking will stop as the person gets older.

WET DREAMS

Wet dreams are one of the most common concerns when entering puberty. During puberty, increases in testosterone can cause the penis to become aroused and ejaculate without direct stimulation. Erections can happen at any time of day or night, even during sleep. Wet dreams, also known as nocturnal emissions, can occur several times in one night. They also may only occur a few times during a person's lifetime. Both scenarios, and any in between, are entirely normal.

As a person's voice drops, it may feel embarrassing to sing or speak in public.

Wet dreams may occur during this time. A wet dream, also known as a nocturnal emission, is when the penis ejaculates semen while the person is asleep. It may or may not be connected to a sexual dream, and the person is not in control of it happening.

During the third Tanner stage, young people grow in height by as much as two to three inches (5 to 7.5 cm) per year.[4] It is also the stage in which they may begin to develop acne on the face and back.

TANNER STAGE FOUR

During the fourth Tanner stage, puberty is in full swing. Breasts are no longer buds, and they grow into a fuller shape. Pubic hair continues to grow. This is also the stage when menstruation begins. It usually starts two to three years after breast buds start to develop. For about six to twelve months before the first period, fluid similar to mucus may discharge from the vagina. Estrogen and progesterone cause the lining of the uterus to thicken and build up in preparation for a fertilized egg. When an egg

BOYS AND BREASTS

All people grow breast tissue during puberty. For cisgender boys, this can be alarming. They might feel disconnected from their bodies. This breast tissue growth is the result of the body turning some testosterone into estrogen, the sex hormone responsible for breast growth. Overweight or obese teens may also have more fat tissue on their chests that makes their breasts appear larger. Fat tissue contains an enzyme that converts testosterone into estrogen. Because of this, overweight boys may produce more estrogen in their fat tissue than boys who are not overweight. This unwanted breast growth during puberty usually goes away in a year or two. When it doesn't, and the breasts become unnaturally large, boys may choose to undergo plastic surgery to reduce their size.

doesn't implant, this lining breaks down and exits the body through the vagina. This is a period. A typical menstrual cycle lasts approximately 28 days, which means that periods happen about once per month. It can take two to three years for menstrual cycles to settle into a regular pattern, and girls might go months between periods or have two within three weeks. Periods can also cause cramps or back pain.

During stage four, the testicles, penis, and scrotum will continue to get bigger, and the scrotum will get darker in color. A boy's voice deepens and becomes permanent so that cracking isn't happening as often or at all. Armpit and pubic hair will grow and thicken, and acne may appear on young people's faces and backs.

> "I HAD REALLY BAD ACNE WHEN I WAS 11 OR 12 YEARS OLD. IT WAS HEART-RENDING AND PEOPLE MADE FUN OF ME. PEOPLE WHISPERED WHEN I WALKED BY IN THE HALLWAYS AND I WAS SURE THEY WERE WHISPERING ABOUT ME. MY ADULT PERSPECTIVE IS MAYBE THEY WEREN'T."[5]
>
> —RAE CARSON, WRITER

TANNER STAGE FIVE

Stage five marks reaching physical maturity. Breasts are close to their full-grown size and shape, although they might continue to change throughout people's lifetimes as they gain or lose weight. Periods may start to become more regular, and pubic hair has grown and filled out to reach the inner thighs. The hips, thighs, and buttocks have also filled out into the rough shape they will be in adulthood, and people are approaching their full adult heights. At this stage, the reproductive system is fully developed and capable of carrying a baby to full term.

Similarly, the penis and scrotum have also reached their full adult size, and pubic hair around the area has filled in and thickened. This hair may also extend across the thighs or up to the navel. Facial hair may also begin to grow, and people may choose to start shaving this hair. The Tanner stages illustrate the rapid physical changes that happen during puberty. Those physical changes come with the need to be prepared for how to deal with all the new things that are occurring.

Caregivers can explain how to use menstrual products to help their children handle the changes in their bodies.

BEING PREPARED

The physical changes that affect children as they grow into adults can be overwhelming and often unexpected. These body changes may mean teens need new ways of coping as they enter adulthood. As breasts develop, teens may be more comfortable wearing bras. Some may want to wear bras as young as eight years old, while others might not start until they are 14 years old. Many begin wearing bras as soon as breast buds develop to the point of becoming visible through the fabric of a shirt. For those who are active or participate in sports, sports bras help keep the breasts comfortable during high-intensity activities such as running and jumping.

It's easy for menstruation to catch someone off guard, especially in the teen years, when periods may be irregular. Many teens carry menstruation supplies such as pads and tampons in their bags or backpacks. This helps them avoid emergencies that may stain or ruin their clothes. Pediatrician Cara Natterson explains, "The biggest lesson is be prepared for the mishaps. When you're younger, periods take you by surprise."[1] Natterson recommends that people add small pouches to their

CHOICES

Many options exist for managing menstrual bleeding. These choices include disposable sanitary pads, reusable cloth pads, tampons, period panties, and menstrual cups. Disposable sanitary pads are worn between the vulva and a pair of underwear. Many people often begin with disposable sanitary pads. Reusable cloth pads are designed to be washed and used again, rather than thrown away after each use.

Teens may also choose to wear tampons. Tampons are absorbent and inserted into the vagina. They absorb menstrual fluid internally. Another internal option is a menstrual cup. A menstrual cup has a bell shape and is made of silicone. Like tampons, menstrual cups are inserted into the vagina to collect menstrual fluid. Menstrual cups can be washed and reused for multiple cycles. Regardless of collection method, menstrual items need to be changed multiple times each day. The specific number depends on the collection method and the heaviness of a person's bleeding.

backpacks with clean underwear and extra menstrual supplies. She emphasizes that people should "never have to worry about how they're going to manage their periods."[2]

It is also helpful to learn how to create an emergency sanitary pad from toilet paper and know which sanitary supplies the school nurse has available. Friends who are already having periods can also be resources in emergency situations. Natterson says that support from friends can be crucial to helping young people understand their bodies and their menstrual cycles. She notes that if a teen notices someone leaking or having a period emergency, the teen should be supportive. "Even someone who's not a good friend. Say, 'Hey, follow me to the bathroom,' or hand her a sweatshirt and tell her to tie it around [her] waist. Do something you would want someone to do for you."[3]

A NEW BODY

During puberty, bodies grow very quickly. Young people experience growth spurts, suddenly adding several inches in height. It may happen so fast that it feels like they are growing overnight. They'll also gain weight as they grow into their adult bodies.

UNEXPECTED ERECTIONS

Unexpected erections can happen during puberty. They can occur in any situation, whether or not the person is aroused or thinking about sex. They may happen while giving a speech in class, talking to a crush, watching a movie at home with family, or in any public place. While there is no way to prevent unexpected erections, it can be helpful to walk around, think about something distracting such as a crossword puzzle or word problem, or conceal the erection with a backpack or sweatshirt. Over the course of puberty, these erections happen less and less frequently.

> "FOR ME, BODY HAIR IS ANOTHER OPPORTUNITY FOR WOMEN TO EXERCISE THEIR ABILITY TO CHOOSE—A CHOICE BASED ON HOW THEY WANT TO FEEL AND THEIR ASSOCIATIONS WITH HAVING OR NOT HAVING BODY HAIR."[4]
>
> —EMILY RATAJKOWSKI, MODEL

Body image becomes a huge factor during puberty, as these changes become noticeable, and teens often begin comparing themselves to others. Body image is the way people feel about their bodies and their looks. For teens, it can be easy to become focused on what they don't like about their new bodies, which can lower their self-esteem.

Not every teen develops at the same rate. Those who develop earlier or later than their peers may be embarrassed about the differences between their bodies and others' bodies. They might look to see who has larger or smaller breasts, or who has larger or smaller muscles.

MORE CHANGES TO COPE WITH

Teens going through puberty will see an increase in hair—not just pubic hair but also hair in their armpits and on their legs, stomachs, chests, and faces. Teens may start shaving their armpits, legs, or faces. They also sweat more, which may lead to body odor and the need to use deodorant.

Teens experience growth spurts at different times, but maintaining healthy, active lifestyles can help improve body image during puberty.

During puberty, teens may start to get acne too. Some teens are lucky and only get a few pimples that go away quickly. But others might have very visible acne that doesn't go away easily. This type of acne is especially hard to deal with at a time when teens are very concerned with body image and comparing themselves to others. Due to hormone fluctuations, acne breakouts can also occur at certain points in the menstrual cycle.

Doctors classify acne as mild, moderate, or severe. Acne is also classified as inflammatory or noninflammatory. Noninflammatory acne usually shows up as pimples or blackheads. People

BOOSTING BODY IMAGE

One of the most difficult things about puberty is struggling with body image as bodies change and develop and there's a greater emphasis on physical appearance. But there are some things that teens can do to help develop a positive body image. One of the most important is to find things to like about one's own looks. Teens should try to focus on what they like about their bodies more than what they don't like. They should also focus on what their bodies can do, such as run, walk, or swim, rather than what they look like.

Self-image also improves when teens take care of their bodies. This includes eating healthfully, refusing drugs and alcohol, getting enough sleep, keeping clean, and taking care of teeth, skin, and hair. Having good self-image also means appreciating oneself on the inside. For example, one can practice mindfulness or journaling to improve one's self-image.

Some creams can help reduce the redness
and painfulness of pimples.

with mild acne usually have blackheads or whiteheads. The
scientific term for these is *comedones*. They occur when
skin pores get clogged. The dark color of blackheads has
nothing to do with dirt. They look dark because inside the

DEALING WITH ACNE

Acne is one of the most difficult aspects of puberty because it is impossible to hide. It also may drastically affect a person's self-esteem. While acne is a normal part of puberty, there are some basic things teens can do to help control breakouts. Having a clean face prevents bacteria and dirt from entering the pores and causing more pustules. Teens can wash their faces with mild soap and warm water twice a day, being careful not to scrub too hard. Additionally, while it may be tempting to pop pimples, this may cause acne to get worse. According to dermatologist Sejal Shah, "As you press on the pimple, you are introducing bacteria and dirt from your finger into the zit. That can cause the pimple to become more red, inflamed, swollen, and infected."[5] Other methods for reducing pimple outbreaks include keeping hands away from the face, regularly cleaning headbands and hats, and avoiding oil-based makeup products. For severe acne, teens should see a dermatologist, who may write a prescription for acne medication.

blackheads, the skin pigment melanin reacts with oxygen in the air. Whiteheads are closed, so they have white or yellowish heads. The more that oil builds up, the more likely it is that bacteria will multiply, which could lead to inflammatory acne. People with moderate acne will have more noticeable pimples. When they get inflamed, the general term *pimples* is actually broken down into two specific categories: papules (small bumps) or pustules (filled with yellow pus). People with severe acne not only have many papules and pustules but also develop reddish, painful nodules, which are hard lumps under the skin. Severe acne often leaves scars that last into adulthood.

Many physical changes come with puberty. Teens learn strategies to help them cope with these changes. But there are other changes as well, such as having to deal with emotions and changing perspectives about oneself and others.

During puberty, teens may feel rapid mood swings, including sudden bouts of anger or sadness.

CHAPTER FIVE

MENTAL AND EMOTIONAL CHANGES

Puberty brings new opportunities as well as increased responsibilities and independence. Trying to be a more independent person and facing new responsibilities and difficulties can be extremely stressful. Teens may find that their relationships with their parents or other trusted adults become strained. They may find that they disagree with their caregivers on various issues. School performance and extracurricular activities are other sources of stress. Some teens also begin the process of researching college options or career paths. There may be changes to relationships with parents as teens seek more independence, and there may be more frequent clashes between teens and their parents. These stressors can make it feel like their emotions are all over the place, up one minute and down the next.

CHANGING HORMONES

Some of the emotions that come with puberty are due to those same chemical messengers that started the whole process: hormones. These hormones produce not only physical changes but emotional changes as well. Hormones such as testosterone and estrogen can be responsible for mood swings, which is when moods can rapidly change from happy and excited to gloomy and sad with very little transition.

Hormones can create feelings of irritability, aggression, depression, and recklessness. These fluctuations often occur during the menstrual cycle right before menstruation starts. In this situation, they are called premenstrual syndrome (PMS). However, all teens experience mood swings, regardless of sex.

CHANGING RELATIONSHIPS

Relationships with parents or other authority figures often become more difficult as teens gain more independence from their caregivers. Teens also tend to take risks that adults would not. They often think impulsively, doing what feels right or good to them at the moment without considering the consequences. When adults try to help teens make good decisions based on their own experiences, some teens react negatively and don't listen to what they are being told. It can be frustrating for caregivers in the situation too, as they may not know how to talk to their teens about these problems. According to neuroscientist Dr. Frances E. Jensen,

It's important to remember that even though their brains are learning at peak efficiency, much else is inefficient, including attention,

COPING WITH MOODINESS

Many teens experience sudden mood swings during puberty, but these mood swings don't have to rule a teen's life. If a mood swing happens, it is helpful to catch one's breath, count to ten slowly, or do something for a few moments that allows one to settle down. It is also helpful to talk to trusted people, especially friends. Friends can help each other by sharing that they are not alone in the feelings they are experiencing.

Physically, it is helpful to get regular exercise, which produces more beta-endorphin, a hormone that controls stress and improves mood. It is also important to get enough sleep because tiredness can lead to more irritability and sadness. And quite simply, crying can also make a teen feel better. Creating something is also helpful, whether that be through writing a diary or journal, producing a piece of music or art, or even constructing something made of wood or cloth. A bad mood might come on for no good reason, but it can also pass on its own.

Between the ages of 11 and 14, the brain reaches its full size. It also has a great deal of plasticity. This means that the brain can adapt to many different things. Participating in school, extracurricular activities, and exercise can help teen brains mature.

While teen brains may have reached their full sizes, they have not yet reached full maturity. The process of developing and maturing is not complete until the mid- to late 20s. The last part of the brain to mature is the front part, known as the prefrontal cortex (PFC). According to the National Institute of Mental Health (NIMH), the PFC "is responsible for skills like planning, prioritizing, and controlling impulses."[3] During early adulthood, the connection between the PFC and the amygdala strengthens. The amygdala is responsible for emotions. Since the PFC will not be fully mature until years after puberty has begun, teens may engage in risky

Before a teen's brain finishes developing, he or she may engage in risky or illegal behavior without fully considering the consequences.

Most teens feel peer pressure to fit in with their friends and classmates. They begin to relate more to their friends than to their caregivers.

behaviors, using their amygdala, without thinking about the potential risks or consequences, using their PFC.

Adolescents also begin to create intimate relationships with their friends and peers around this time. This can emotionally distance them from their caregivers. Additionally, their self-image is closely influenced by how they think other people, especially their peers, see them. Feelings of insecurity, as well as pressure from peers, society, and the media, suddenly make it very important for teens to fit in with a crowd. They may want to feel accepted or popular among their classmates. They may change how they dress, speak, or behave during puberty. Teens are more likely to be influenced by their friends, as well as popular culture and the media, than their parents or caregivers. These influences help shape who each person will be as an adult. According to psychologist Dr. Carl E. Pickhardt:

> To begin the separation from childhood (and from parents and family) that starts adolescence, the young person has to reject some of

THE SELFIE GENERATION

Social media platforms, such as Twitter, Instagram, and TikTok, have become a common form of communication. However, social media can have a huge negative impact on body image. Studies addressing the relationship between social media and adolescent body image have found that selfies posted on social media, where other people can "like" an image or express some other form of positive or negative reaction, give teens a chance to earn approval from their peers about how they look. However, this feedback may sometimes have a negative effect on how teens see themselves. Researchers Ilyssa Salomon and Christia Spears Brown authored a 2018 study on teens, body image, and social media use. They wrote, "Spending a lot of time on social media taking and posting selfies is associated with thinking about their bodies more frequently and thinking more negatively about their bodies."[4] The researchers also noted that some teens who already feel societal pressure to look a certain way may be more at risk for these negative effects of social media.

*the old lifestyle that branded him or her as "child,"
thus freeing up growing room for the journey to
independence ahead. Through attitude and actions
the young person is saying, "I no longer want to be
defined and treated as a child anymore."*[5]

The struggle to fit in with friends and peers can create conflict with teens' caregivers, especially if fitting in with peers goes against something important to their caregivers, such as religious or political beliefs. In addition, there are pressures brought on by social media, such as representations of how teens think they are supposed to look or act. These give teens a new platform to not only gauge themselves against other teens but also ostracize, criticize, and bully others. These pressures affect both teens' relationships with parents as well as their general mental health.

MENTAL HEALTH

Emotions such as irritability, boredom, or hopelessness can be signs of depression. Depression isn't just about general sad feelings or being indifferent or angry. It is a clinical diagnosis by a mental health professional. The symptoms of depression can include feeling sad, anxious, or empty; feeling worthless or helpless; and losing interest in hobbies and activities. Teens can also suffer from anxiety, which is characterized by excessive worry, fear, or

Teens with ADHD may find it difficult to pay attention to schoolwork, extracurricular activities, and plans with friends.

uneasiness. Eating disorders also become more common. Some teens also suffer from attention deficit hyperactivity disorder (ADHD), which is characterized by inattention or hyperactivity that interferes with daily functioning or development.

If teens are experiencing any of these mental health symptoms and they begin to get in the way of enjoying life or interacting with friends and family, then it could be a serious condition and not just teenage hormones.

SEX IN THE MEDIA

According to the University of Washington website Let's Talk Teens, Sexuality, & Media, kids and teens in the United States are exposed to a huge amount of sex in the media. Media is no longer simply entertainment. It can also have an enormous effect on the attitudes and behaviors of children and teens as they are developing. It can contribute to an early start of sexual activity as well as affect self-image and body dissatisfaction by creating unrealistic expectations for beauty. These can contribute to eating disorders. However, these influences are increasingly difficult to avoid. According to Let's Talk Teens, Sexuality, & Media, teens in the United States spend more than seven hours per day consuming different types of media, which often contain sexual content. For example, teen magazines such as *Seventeen* and *Teen Vogue* "devote an average of two to five pages per issue to sexual topics."[6] Additionally, many teens get information about sex and body image from the internet, some of which may be harmful or inaccurate.

This is especially true if symptoms bring on feelings of wanting to hurt oneself. Teens who think they might be suffering from any of these disorders should talk to a counselor, therapist, or other trusted adult.

ROMANTIC AND SEXUAL FEELINGS

Friendships are important to teens going through puberty. Puberty is a time when teens may start to think about sexual and romantic relationships as well. The process of moving toward sexual maturity means teens may have a great deal of curiosity

about those whom they find attractive. Even something
that used to be an everyday activity, such as watching a
movie or reading a romantic book or listening to music,
may now bring on feelings of sexual excitement or arousal.
The media is also filled with sexual content and images,
and girls especially are bombarded with images of clothing,
makeup, and hairstyles that are all supposed to make
them sexier.

Sexual feelings bring many, many questions. It is very
important that as tweens and teens are going through
puberty and starting to experience sexual feelings,
they are provided with accurate information about sex,
reproduction, and sexual
health. Many young
people receive some
of this information at
school. According to
a survey by the US
Centers for Disease
Control and Prevention
(CDC), 96 to 97 percent
of teenagers surveyed
received formal sex
education before they
were 18.[8] But not every school has health or sex education
classes. Information about sex from friends or the internet

may not be accurate. It might feel extremely embarrassing to ask a parent questions such as "How will I know when I'm ready to have sex?" or "What do I do if my boyfriend or girlfriend is pressuring me to have sex?"

Questions about sexual orientation or gender identity may also be uncomfortable. But a caregiver or trusted adult is the best place to start for accurate information. Even if having a conversation is too difficult, they can help find reputable sources of information.

Many LGBTQ teens discover their sexuality and gender identity as they go through puberty.

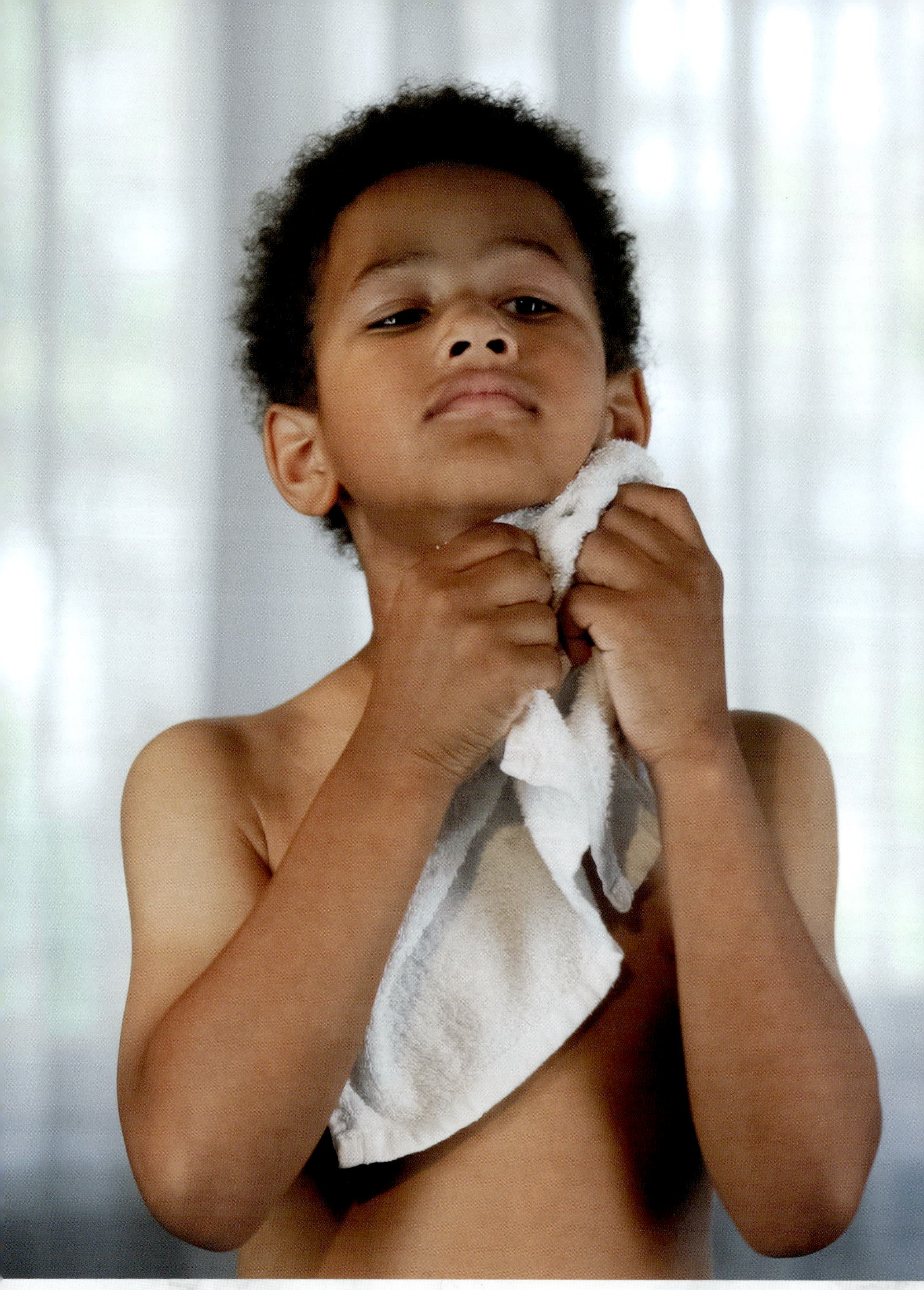

Children who go through precocious puberty may notice changes earlier than the Tanner stages say they should appear.

TOO EARLY? TOO LATE?

Even though puberty looks different for every person, it should happen during specific age ranges in order to progress normally. If puberty starts too early or too late, health-care providers may want to look into reasons why. Sometimes, people require medication or other treatments depending on these types of puberty.

PRECOCIOUS PUBERTY

When puberty begins before ages eight or nine, health-care providers refer to it as precocious puberty. It is a rare condition, affecting less than 1 percent of the US population.[1] The word *precocious* indicates that a child is developing abilities or attributes much sooner than usual. These include bones and muscles that grow more rapidly than usual for the child's age. The reproductive system may be developing too early as well.

Patrick Burleigh was a child who went through precocious puberty. Burleigh felt like precocious puberty affected many aspects of his childhood and adolescence.

Later in life, he wrote about his experience with precocious puberty:

> *I was . . . considerably bigger . . . than a 2-year-old, and also [had] impulsive behavior that's characteristic of someone going through puberty. . . . You know, an inability to control my impulses, aggressive outbursts, hitting other kids, tantrums that were kind of truly epic—just behavior that was extreme. . . . At my first [doctor's] visit, I was about 3 years old and I weighed as much and was as tall as a 7-year-old, and had the testosterone levels of a 14-year-old.[2]*

Doctors diagnose patients with precocious puberty by starting with the family's medical history. X-rays of the child's hands and wrists can help the doctor determine bone age, a measure of the maturity of a child's skeleton. Determining a child's bone age tells the doctor if the bones are growing too quickly. The doctor will also perform a test called a GnRH stimulation test to diagnose which form of precocious puberty the child has.

Treatment for precocious puberty varies. Sometimes, if there's no identifiable cause, there will be no treatment other than to monitor the child's progress. Other treatments include injections of medication that delays further development. The injections will stop when the child reaches the normal age for puberty, and then the natural process can resume.

CENTRAL OR PERIPHERAL

There are two types of precocious puberty: central and peripheral. With central precocious puberty, the cause for the condition is often unidentifiable. The process starts too soon, but once it begins, the progress of puberty and the steps that are part of development typically happen with normal timing in a normal pattern. In some rare cases, central precocious puberty is caused by ailments such as tumors, cancer, spinal cord injuries, or genetic disorders. But in

RISK FACTORS

Some risk factors that may lead to precocious puberty are genetic or linked to ethnicity, and others are environmental. Children with uteruses are more likely to develop precocious puberty, and children who are Black are also affected more often than children of other races. Being obese, which is defined as being 30 pounds or more above the average weight for a particular height, can also make precocious puberty more likely. Certain medical conditions are also risk factors. A child who has had radiation treatment for a condition of the central nervous system, such as leukemia, is also at higher risk. Also, coming into contact with sex hormones, such as touching an adult's creams or ointments that contain certain hormones, also creates risk.[3]

There isn't much that can be done to prevent most forms of precocious puberty except to make sure that adult medications and treatments containing hormones are kept away from young children. It is also a good idea for parents to help children maintain healthy weights and avoid becoming obese.

If children show signs of precocious puberty, health-care providers can help determine the cause.

many cases of central precocious puberty, there is no definable reason.

The second type, peripheral precocious puberty, occurs due to increased levels of estrogen or testosterone in a child's body. Typically during puberty, GnRH signals the brain to begin puberty, which then triggers estrogen and testosterone production from the gonads. However, during peripheral precocious puberty, estrogen and testosterone enter the body because of specific problems or diseases. These problems can include tumors in the adrenal or pituitary glands, ovaries, or testicles, as well as genetic disorders. Additionally, children may be exposed to external sources of estrogen or testosterone, such as creams or ointments that are prescribed to adults for various medical conditions. Health-care providers may run tests to look for disorders that can cause precocious puberty, such as polycystic ovarian syndrome (PCOS) or certain types of cancer.

Precocious puberty of either kind can bring certain complications, both physical and emotional. While children with precocious puberty may grow very quickly and be taller

RARE CAUSES OF PRECOCIOUS PUBERTY

There are a few extremely rare genetic syndromes that can cause precocious puberty. One is McCune-Albright syndrome, a disorder that affects the bones, skin, and several hormone-producing (endocrine) tissues. In addition to causing precocious puberty, it also changes the body's bone structure, causing increasing pain and physical deformity, as well as changes in skin pigmentation. McCune-Albright syndrome occurs in fewer than 0.001 percent of people.[4] Neurofibromatosis (NF) is another genetic disorder with highly variable manifestations, including precocious puberty, which can affect many body systems. In addition to precocious puberty, it can cause multiple nerve tumors to grow under the skin, which can result in disfigurement, curvature of the spine and long bones, and other complications. The condition often becomes more active during puberty, as well as pregnancy and menopause. NF occurs in fewer than 0.25 percent of births.[5]

BLOCKING PUBERTY

Some transgender and gender diverse preteens may use prescription medications called puberty blockers to temporarily suppress the start of puberty. Puberty can cause a great deal of distress for preteens who are gender nonconforming, and puberty blockers can give them more time to understand their gender identity. It can also give children and their families time to prepare for some of the medical, emotional, developmental, social, and legal issues that are ahead.

Puberty-blocking medications suppress the body's release of sex hormones that affect the body's primary and secondary sexual characteristics. For those identified as males at birth, puberty blockers decrease the growth of facial and body hair, prevent voice deepening, and limit the growth of the genitalia. For those identified as female at birth, treatment limits or stops breast development and delays or stops menstruation. Teens only take puberty blockers for a few years before either choosing to stop or pursuing another form of hormone therapy.

than their friends of the same age, they may also stop growing earlier than usual. This means that once they reach adulthood, they could be shorter than most other adults. Emotionally, being fairly young children who are suddenly developing like people much older can make them feel self-conscious around their friends of the same age. They might be embarrassed or ashamed of the changes happening to their bodies that aren't yet happening to anyone else around them. It's possible that this could lead to poor self-esteem and even depression. According to Jane Mendle, a psychologist at Cornell University, "As children develop physically, it changes how they think about themselves and how people relate to them socially."[6] Mendle added that girls who mature early have an increased risk of psychosocial problems, such as inappropriate or early sexual behavior.

These young people may also receive different treatment from older children and adults. People may view them as more mature than they are because of how their bodies look. This may lead to unwanted and inappropriate sexual advances. Boys can also be affected.

The age at which menstruation begins in Western cultures has been decreasing for decades. For example, in the early 1900s, the average age for the onset of menstruation was 16 to 17 years old. Today, it is around age 12 or 13.[7] Scientists aren't sure of the reason, although some believe it's due to hormones in children's environments. In 2012, a study conducted by the CDC showed that the average onset of menstruation was seven months earlier for children who were exposed to high levels of certain household chemicals than children who were not exposed.[8]

Chemicals known to be hormone or endocrine disruptors mimic or interfere with the body's natural hormones and the endocrine system. These chemicals are found in everyday products such as plastic bottles and

Some plastic water bottles contain BPA, a chemical that may affect when a child begins puberty.

containers, detergent, toys, cosmetics, and pesticides. These chemicals include bisphenol A (BPA), which is found in plastics, and triclosan, which is found in antibacterial personal products such as body wash. People come into contact with these chemicals through their diets, the air, their skin, and water. Because early puberty can increase risks for breast cancer, ovarian cancer, obesity, diabetes, and emotional issues in adult life such as depression,

scientists are trying to determine what factors are causing
it and how they can be controlled.

DELAYED PUBERTY

Some teens also begin puberty much later than average.
This is known as delayed puberty. Signs and symptoms
of delayed puberty include a lack of breast development
by age 13, a lack of menstruation by age 16, and a lack of
testicle growth by age 14.

Delayed puberty is not an emergency condition, but
a child who has not begun puberty within the normal age
range should see a health-care provider to make sure that
there are no underlying health conditions. It is not clear
whether delayed puberty affects genders differently, but
health-care providers
report that caregivers are
often more concerned
when boys do not keep up
with their peers in height
and development.

Delayed puberty
can be a source of
emotional distress for
teens because they are
not keeping up with
their peers at a time

"DELAYED PUBERTY CAN BE
EXTREMELY EMBARRASSING
AND DISTRESSING AND, IN
SOME CASES, CAN HAVE
HEALTH CONSEQUENCES, SUCH
AS BONE PROBLEMS FROM
PROLONGED GROWTH."[9]

—RICHARD SHARPE,
ENDOCRINOLOGY EXPERT

when body image and physical comparisons are huge issues. Late puberty can create feelings of isolation and withdrawal, poor relationships with peers, poor body image, a loss of self-esteem, anxiety about what will happen in the future and about not fitting in, and even depression. Over the long term, it may mean a loss of social and developmental opportunities.

CAUSES OF DELAYED PUBERTY

Sometimes teens will start puberty later than their peers, simply because everyone develops at a different rate. For example, elite athletes may experience delayed puberty because they have a lower body fat percentage than other children. But there are also medical reasons why delayed puberty occurs. One reason is a condition called constitutional growth delay (CGD). CGD describes children who are growing at a normal rate but are small for their age. Their bone age is younger than their actual age in years. Children with CGD don't have any diseases that inhibit growth. They simply grow more slowly. CGD also tends to be an

Some athletes, such as ballerinas, may experience delayed puberty because of their intense training schedules.

inherited condition. If a child's parents reached puberty later, then chances are good that the child will be the same way in his or her own growth patterns. But children with CGD, since they start growing later, will also continue to grow for a longer period of time. This means that they will still be growing when most of their peers have stopped growing. Eventually they will catch up and reach a normal adult height.

Other underlying medical conditions, as well as certain medications, can cause delayed puberty. Celiac disease is a disorder in which eating gluten proteins triggers an immune response; this affects children's ability to gain weight because of damage to the small intestine. Because their bodies can't absorb nutrients well, they don't grow and develop at the same rate as their peers. This delays the onset of puberty. Eating disorders such as anorexia and bulimia also delay puberty because the body does not receive enough nutrients. And, any condition that

People with celiac disease cannot eat foods containing gluten, such as pasta and bread. However, many grocery stores carry gluten-free versions of these foods.

prevents the ovaries or testes from responding to hormonal signals for starting puberty can result in delayed puberty.

Most of the time, delayed puberty does not require medical intervention. Often, a child's body will begin developing on its own. Occasionally a doctor might prescribe short-term hormone therapy to jump-start puberty. This takes the form of hormone pills, patches, or injections. Most of the time, once puberty does begin, there won't be any other effects on growth or fertility as adults.

Sooner or later, nearly all tweens and teens will go through puberty, according to their own bodies' schedules. There will be many changes and many new experiences, and they bring with them the need for new coping skills.

One way to help handle the challenge of puberty is to spend time with friends.

CHAPTER SEVEN

HANDLING THE CHANGES

Puberty is one of the biggest challenges that many teens go through. It affects them both physically and emotionally. While some of these changes can feel negative, many can also be quite exciting. Regardless of whether the changes are mental or physical, teens can develop coping skills to handle them and navigate puberty successfully.

HEALTHY AND ACTIVE LIFESTYLES

One way to handle the changes of puberty is to adopt a healthy lifestyle. This might mean increasing physical activity, getting plenty of sleep, eating nutritious foods, and having good personal hygiene. These basics are not only a way to maintain a healthy body but are also good habits to build for a lifetime of healthy living.

Teens going through puberty usually have an increased appetite and need more food. Their bodies are burning more calories than ever before as they grow. Balanced diets can help teens keep their bodies healthy and active as they go through their growth spurts. They also help teens build muscles.

Family members can encourage each other to
stay active and live healthy lifestyles.

When teens enter puberty, their caloric needs change.
Some teens need between 2,500 and 3,000 calories a day.[1]
Teens who are active and move around a great deal, such
as those playing sports, may require more calories, while
those who are sedentary, or less active, require fewer. Junk
food that is high in fat and sugar will quickly pile on calories

with little nutritional benefit. A healthy diet gives the body more nutrients while consuming calories.

EATING DISORDERS

Puberty is also a time when body image in comparison to peers and images in the media can lead to dissatisfaction with a person's self-image. It also makes puberty one of the riskiest times for developing an eating disorder such as anorexia or bulimia. These can lead to behaviors like binge eating, purging, dieting, and obsessing over weight.

SIGNS OF AN EATING DISORDER

The signs and symptoms of an eating disorder vary, depending on what kind of disorder a teen has. These signs can include excessive worry about weight gain and a rigid or even severe diet that doesn't provide the body with enough nutrients. Some girls with eating disorders may stop menstruating, which is a sign of starvation and can cause lasting physical damage.

Obsession with physical appearance and how others perceive the teen's body can also be a warning sign. Someone with an eating disorder may want to eat alone to avoid others seeing what the teen is or isn't eating. People with eating disorders may use the bathroom often after meals to hide the fact that they might be forcing themselves to throw up. Any unhealthy and repeated actions to lose or even gain weight, including overexercising, are warning signs, as well as experiencing unusual stress or discomfort about eating habits.[2]

Teens can develop eating disorders for many different reasons, although the exact cause might be unknown. One major risk factor is pressure from society and popular culture to be thin. This pressure often makes even teens at healthy weights feel as if they are overweight and may trigger obsessions with dieting and weight loss. Other factors include activities such as modeling or elite athletics, which value being lean and thin. Finally, some teens have genetic or biological factors that make them more likely to develop eating disorders. Personality traits such as perfectionism, anxiety, or a tendency to be rigid and dislike change can also influence eating disorders.

It is very important for parents and teens

READING CUES

Researchers have found that one of the reasons why teens have difficulty communicating well with their parents and other adults is the way in which their brains work. When it comes to perceiving emotion, such as reading facial expressions to tell how someone is feeling, teens tend to use a part of the brain called the amygdala, a small, almond-shaped region that governs instinctive reactions. Adults use the frontal cortex of their brains to read emotions, an area that governs reason and planning. This means that teens are not only misreading emotions but also strongly reacting to them. The frontal cortex, which adults use, gives them the ability to distinguish more subtle emotions and respond to them with reason. As teens get older, this function starts to shift toward the frontal cortex and away from the amygdala.

to be aware of behaviors that might indicate an eating disorder. It is also important for teens to help friends if they see them exhibiting these behaviors. A school counselor or a family physician can help teens deal with eating disorders and get the help they need.

COPING WITH OTHER PHYSICAL CHANGES

Other physical aspects of puberty, such as increased body odor, beard growth, acne, and menstrual periods, will require good personal hygiene to cope with successfully and to avoid embarrassment. Teens need to keep clean by showering, using deodorant, shaving, and treating acne with skin-care products or a dermatologist's help. It can take a while for teens to realize that they might have greasy hair or body odor, and if a parent or friend calls their attention to it, it's a good, gentle reminder to begin handling their own personal hygiene.

Teens experience facial changes too. For some, the chin lengthens and the nose thickens. This happens as the bone, cartilage, and muscle underneath the face change. Diet and environment also affect growth. Teens who have had poor diets or have not had access to good medical care will not reach the same height and weight as teens who have had healthy lifestyles, good health care, and nutrition.

Metabolism fluctuates during puberty as well. There are times when rapid growth spurts require fuel for the body, which increases metabolism and requires more calories than normal. About 25 percent of the body's growth happens during puberty, so the body needs those extra calories to form the muscle, bone, fat, and other tissues that make that growth possible.[3] Once the body is fully grown, the metabolism slows down, and the body will require fewer calories.

EXPERIENCING INTENSE EMOTIONS

It is a common expression to say that puberty is an emotional roller-coaster ride. It is possible to be wildly happy one moment, be incredibly depressed the next, and then flare up with rebelliousness or anger. Teens are famous for exhibiting sullen moods, sudden outbursts, and impulsive actions. These wild mood swings are caused in part by the new hormones coursing through a teen's body, as well as the growing need for independence and self-discovery.

While puberty is a time when many teens find increased independence, they still need support from caregivers and other trusted adults.

Teens deal with a wide variety of emotions as they leave childhood and move toward becoming adults. There is frustration from seeking more freedom and being impatient with not being old enough to do what they want. There is anger when it doesn't feel like they are being treated fairly or when they are being embarrassed. All of the new opportunities and experiences opening up during puberty can cause anxiety, but they can also bring excitement and curiosity about new adventures. Embarrassment is a huge emotion for teens because they are increasingly sensitive and self-conscious about their changing bodies. There can be confusion about how their worlds are becoming more complex, which also creates feelings of stress. There can also be sadness in leaving childhood behind. The need to compete and be challenged as they get older can bring disappointment. There is also boredom from not yet being allowed to act like adults and having to keep doing things that they dislike, as well as loneliness as teens become less reliant on their families and parents.

> "IN VERY BASIC TERMS WHAT HAPPENS DURING PUBERTY IS YOUR BRAIN REALLY REMODELS. THE END PRODUCT IS DIFFERENT."[4]
>
> —LAURA PEREIRA, RESEARCHER

Often, these emotions come out in interactions between teens and their caregivers. Teens may not want to have conversations with their caregivers because it is easy to feel irritated by what a caregiver says. Teens may feel like they no longer want to be treated like children. It is common to want to rebel against what their caregivers say, especially if a teen no longer agrees with their points of view. Teens should feel free to simply tell their caregivers that they just want to be listened to and that they aren't asking for caregivers to solve their problems for them.

However, caregivers should know what is going on with their teens. They should be aware if something has happened that their teens need help with or that is causing harm to their children. They should also know if their teens are extremely unhappy. For teens, talking with their caregivers can be good practice in being honest and straightforward with their feelings. This is a skill that they can use throughout their lives. It also shows their caregivers that they are ready for mature, responsible discussions. According to psychologist Dr. Carl Pickhardt, "By talking, he or she puts into spoken words what he or she is experiencing, feeling, thinking, wanting and not wanting, and then verbally conveying this message to parents."[5] Learning to speak up is much better than adopting the habit of being noncommunicative, which may generate feelings of isolation and loneliness.

During puberty, many teens feel irritated or exasperated by their caregivers. But communicating with caregivers is one way to make sure that teens are healthy and safe.

ROLE CHANGES

Many of the thoughts that teens have to deal with during puberty are related to the cognitive changes taking place in their brains. Unlike children, teens begin to think in abstract terms, about concepts that are less concrete. They are becoming able to consider multiple points of view beyond their own and to look at all the possibilities within a situation. They can begin to think hypothetically and use logical thought processes. However, this process of learning how to reason, argue, and respond, especially with adults, means that they will also frequently challenge adults. And, because they don't yet have the life experience or context to solve problems as well as adults, and because their brains have not yet fully finished developing, they can't always make solid decisions.

In addition to these cognitive changes, teens going through puberty are also beginning to understand how different people play different roles in life and that they themselves are going to be playing different roles as they become adults. They begin to question their own identities and may test different personas to find one that fits. Teens also start to express their own opinions and may embrace certain causes or ideas while rejecting others. While these are all good signs of evolving into adults, trying to build a new sense of personal identity can cause additional stress on top of the other changes taking place during puberty.

COPING WITH STRESS

There are ways for teens who are going through puberty to cope with some of the stress in their lives. The first thing is to recognize the signs of that stress. These signs may include crying, angry outbursts, difficulty sleeping, and withdrawing from others. Teens may also experience stomachaches and headaches, as well as anxiety or nervousness that doesn't go away. Some may also feel

CAUSES OF STRESS

There are many causes of stress for teens. In a 2018 poll of teens conducted by the American Psychological Association (APA), 91 percent of respondents said they experienced "at least one physical or emotional symptom due to stress in the past month." When asked the same question, only 74 percent of adults experienced at least one symptom.[6] The APA survey found that teens were stressed about topics in national news stories, such as gun violence, immigration, and the future of the country. Other sources included school performance, extracurricular activities, and family obligations or responsibilities.

Teens face a lot of pressure, whether it's the pressure to find romantic partners, to get into their dream colleges, or to make enough money at their after-school jobs to help support their families. They also feel pressure to fit in with their peers, perhaps by dressing in certain ways, having certain body shapes, or experimenting with drugs and alcohol. Additionally, puberty itself is a source of stress.

the urge to try drugs and alcohol to cope with stress.

However, there are many positive strategies for coping with stress. They include talking about problems with others, such as a friend, trusted adult, or caregiver. It also helps to take deep, calming breaths and at the same time think or say aloud, "I can handle this." It is also helpful to practice something called progressive muscle relaxation, which involves repeatedly tensing and relaxing large muscles of the body.

When teens feel overwhelmed by the number of tasks on

their to-do lists, it may help to break those tasks down. For example, a task such as "take care of the dog" may feel overwhelming. However, writing out each of the smaller items, such as "feed the dog," "go on a walk," and "give the dog a bath," may help the task seem more manageable—especially as each item gets crossed off the list.

Other coping strategies include getting exercise, eating regular meals, and getting the proper amount of sleep. It is also vital to schedule study breaks and make time for enjoyable activities. When it seems like there are too many things that can't be controlled, focus on what can be controlled and let go of the things that can't, such as other people's expectations and opinions. Work through worst-case scenarios until they start to seem amusing or even absurd. Most importantly, it is necessary to accept oneself, identify one's own unique strengths, and build on them. Give up on the idea of being perfect. Cultivate the ability to learn from mistakes. It can also be helpful to explore creativity as a means of self-expression. Activities such as music, dance, and art can help with managing stress and also provide ways to explore and express identities.

Teens may experience their first romantic crushes during puberty.

CHAPTER EIGHT

RELATIONSHIPS AND PUBERTY

The part of going through puberty that can be the most stressful, exciting, and complicated is relationships, especially relationships with friends or romantic partners. Friendships may start to become as important as family relationships. Young children tend to make friendships based on shared activities, but teens begin to form friendships not only based on shared activities but also shared values, attitudes, and educational interests. Teens may have intimate conversations with their friends as a way to explore their identities and feelings about sexuality. Alternatively, they may not have these intimate conversations with friends but instead with family members or members of their faith communities.

For most teens, romantic relationships start to become very important, although it's also normal for teens to have no interest in romantic relationships until they reach their late teens, especially if they are very focused on school, hobbies, or sports. Some teens

ABUSIVE RELATIONSHIPS

Some teens may find themselves in abusive relationships. It may be difficult to tell whether a relationship is abusive. According to Planned Parenthood's resources for teens, "If you think you're being treated badly, you probably are. . . . Healthy relationships make you feel good about yourself, not bad." Some signs of abusive relationships include one partner controlling another, hurting a partner physically, and stalking a partner.

Those in abusive relationships should seek help from adults they trust when trying to end a relationship. And teens whose friends are in abusive relationships can start by listening to them, being present, and urging them to ask for help. People experiencing abuse are not alone. Planned Parenthood's resources affirm:

> Abuse is never your fault. It's not right for anyone to hurt you, make you feel bad about yourself, or pressure you to do things you don't want to do. Everyone gets mad sometimes, but talking about it is the way to deal with problems—not hurting you or putting you down.[1]

may never pursue romantic relationships, or they may identify as aromantic, or without romantic attraction.

Interest in relationships often starts with a crush: First is the identity crush, which happens when a teen admires someone and wants to be like the person. Then there are romantic crushes, which often don't last long because the teen sees the object of the crush as being perfect. The crush subsides when the teen realizes that the person is imperfect. Young teens tend to socialize in groups, but eventually many teens reach the point of wanting to date just one person.

IT'S A SOCIAL MEDIA WORLD

One modern aspect of relationships during puberty is the increasing importance of social media in how teens interact with one another. According to a 2018 Pew Research Center survey, 97 percent of teens ages 13 to 17 used some kind of social media platform, such as Twitter, YouTube, and TikTok. Forty-five percent of respondents said they are online almost constantly. Many of the teens in the survey reported that social media use deepens their friendships and makes them feel more connected to their friends' lives and feelings. A majority also reported that it makes them feel more confident, more included, and more outgoing.[2]

SOCIAL MEDIA CONVERSATIONS

One way teens can deal with the negative effects of social media is by setting reasonable limits on social media use, especially at bedtime, when the use of electronics can make it more difficult to fall asleep. Teens can also talk with their caregivers about privacy settings and turning off location-enabled services to make sure that private information isn't shared in places on the internet that can compromise their safety. It is also vital that a teen experiencing any form of cyberbullying report it to a parent or school official. Reporting helps keep teens safe while staying connected through social media.

However, social media can disrupt their sleep, distract them from other tasks such as homework, and give them an unrealistic view of other people's lives, since many people on social media tend to make their lives look better than they actually are. Social media also exposes teens to cyberbullying and peer pressure, and it makes spreading rumors easy. Teens who spend more than three hours a day on social media have been shown to be at a higher risk for mental health problems, such as depression and anxiety.[3] It's also easy to compare oneself to the images and events that are seen when using social media, which can also increase the risk of depression.

SEX AND SEXUALITY

It is important that teens going through puberty have clear, accurate information about birth control, safe sex, and sexually transmitted infections (STIs). Teens often rely on their friends for information about sex rather than their parents, but that information may not necessarily be correct. There are resources for teens to help them get accurate information without having to ask caregivers, which can be embarrassing. It's also important to talk about peer pressure, and especially pressure to have sex before a teen is ready.

While these conversations can potentially be uncomfortable, often parents can be the best sources

Teens can discuss sex and sexuality with their health-care providers. Providers can answer questions about sex, birth control, and hormones.

of information. It is worth developing the ability to have good conversations about difficult subjects. If that's not possible, school counselors and family doctors can also be resources.

LGBTQ RELATIONSHIPS

Puberty is also a time where exploring sexuality might include exploring an attraction to people of the same sex. In fact, between four and 10 percent of people discover that they are sexually attracted to people of the same sex.[4] They may begin to explore this sexual attraction during puberty. Sexuality develops and sometimes shifts over time, and puberty is a time for exploration, which is very common. Just because a teen explores a same-sex relationship now does not necessarily mean they will continue to have same-sex relationships for the rest of their lives.

Teens who identify as part of the lesbian, gay, bisexual, transgender, and queer (LGBTQ) community need to have reliable and accurate information about sex and sexuality. Healthy sex ed, no matter what a teen's sexuality might be, can help reduce risky behavior and the chances or unwanted pregnancy or STIs. It can assist teens with gender identity and sexual orientation questions by giving them medically accurate information that is appropriate for their age group. Most importantly, LGBTQ teens need to be provided with positive examples of LGBTQ individuals, romantic

Couples can research information about sex and sexuality together in order to keep both people healthy and safe.

relationships, and families. People of all sexual identities should be prepared and educated about how to protect themselves during sexual activity.

There are many things to cope with during puberty, and sometimes it can feel like most of them are negative. But in reality, puberty is a gateway to many new and exciting experiences and opportunities. Becoming an adult brings a variety of freedoms, challenges, and responsibilities.

While puberty may feel as though it lasts forever, it does end for all as their bodies mature into adult ones.

CHAPTER NINE

THE FUTURE BEGINS

It would be helpful if there were a definite end to puberty that people could mark on a calendar, sort of like graduating from high school, when a specific day comes and puberty is officially over. Unfortunately, it isn't that neat. Just like the onset of puberty, the end of puberty is different for every single person. On average, puberty ends around age 16, but most variations are perfectly normal.[1] How long puberty lasts can depend on several things.

One factor is family history and genetics, since teens will often experience puberty's beginning and end on a similar schedule to how their parents or siblings experienced it. Personal health and lifestyle can also affect it, with diet, stress levels, and the amount of exercise all contributing. Environment can also have an effect, since some factors such as hormone exposure can trigger early puberty. If puberty begins earlier, it will end earlier too. And hormones themselves regulate when puberty ends. For a late bloomer, who began puberty later than most teens, it will naturally be later in age before puberty ends.

Puberty ends when the body has stopped growing. At this point, the reproductive organs are fully grown, the body has grown hair in the underarms and pubic region, and teens have more or less reached their full adult heights. Breasts will have finished development, and menstruation will have become more regular. Building muscle will happen faster and more easily. Teens will also have developed higher blood pressure to move blood more effectively during growth spurts.

THE ADULT BRAIN

Young adulthood is also a time when cognitive abilities are high. The brain finally reaches full maturity with the development of the prefrontal cortex, which completes brain development. It is a time when young adults have usually gained some kind of expertise in a career or in their education. Psychologist Jean Piaget developed a theory of cognitive development. He theorized that operational thinking is established in young adulthood. Operational thinking includes the ability to think abstractly, use deductive reasoning, and create and test hypotheses.

Some psychologists since Piaget have also identified another stage of thinking, called postformal operational thinking. In this stage, adults make decisions using both logic and emotions. Unlike adolescents, adults learn how to make reasoned responses to situations that are highly charged with emotions.

MARKING THE END OF CHILDHOOD

Some cultures have formal ceremonies and rituals to mark the beginning of adulthood, and these often occur

During a bat mitzvah, a Jewish girl will read Hebrew from the Torah, part of the Hebrew scriptures.

alongside puberty. Jewish children may have a bar mitzvah or bat mitzvah at 12 or 13 years old to signify becoming an adult in their religion. According to the teachings of the Quran, Muslim parents must teach their children about adulthood and responsibilities. As soon as children begin going through puberty, they are seen as being adults in Islam.

In some cultures, teens have to pass a series of tests before they are seen as adults. For example, girls in the

MEDIEVAL CUSTOMS

During the medieval period in Europe, which lasted from 400 CE to 1400 CE, puberty was marked as starting at the point when girls and boys were able to have children. The medieval philosopher Avicenna wrote, "There is the age of growing up, which is called the age of adolescence and commonly lasts until the age of thirty."[3]

However, in actuality medieval society was not so clear about when puberty ended. Women were thought to leave childhood once they were married and left their family households, which happened earlier than it does today. Boys in Europe were thought to be adult enough to consent to marriage at age 14, but they could not legally inherit property until age 21. Young adults may have married earlier, often before age 16, but usually with the understanding that they would probably not live as husband and wife until they were older and developed sexual maturity.

Mescalero Apache Tribe in New Mexico undergo a four-day ceremony to mark their transition from girls to women. When the ceremony ends, each young girl is bathed in yucca root suds before she puts on her adult clothes.[2] Great Plains tribes send boys on vision quests, where they go out into nature and fast for four days and four nights, alone at a sacred site. They hope to receive a vision, which will help them find their purpose in life and their role in their community. Some aboriginal boys in Australia go on long journeys on foot, called walkabouts, where they hone their skills in hunting and tracking.

THE STAGE IS SET

It may be helpful to think of the end of puberty as the beginning of adult life. The stage is being set for teens to become the adults they want to be. Teens have been developing interests that are more abstract, such as social justice or art. They may have started to become passionate about specific causes. This often coincides with the point where they graduate from high school and make decisions about whether to go to college and what

interests and careers to pursue. They are establishing dreams and goals, and they are starting to map out how they will achieve those goals.

Physically, young adults who have gone through puberty are able to reproduce. They have also grown in physical strength and maturity and can fully participate in activities that require strong, capable bodies. Once they have finished growing and adjusting to their new adult bodies, many teens find that they are capable of new achievements in sports or other activities that involve physical strength.

Early adulthood, from approximately ages 20 to 40, is when humans reach their physical peak for muscle strength, heart function, reaction time, and sensory abilities.[5] It is during this stage that many professional athletes are at the heights of their careers. This is also the time when many people start families.

Puberty can be rough, even for those teens who make it look easy, and it can be a roller coaster of emotions, experiences, and challenges. But it is simply the first step that leads to a world filled with choices. Soon, teens will leave high school and start college or a career. They will take on

HEALTHY ADULT BONES

Scientists have found evidence that teens who started their puberty growth spurt at an older age may be at risk for lower bone density as young adults. This means that they have weaker bones in the early years of adulthood. Those who experienced puberty later than most teens also had lower bone density at the spine and hips, places which are known to be susceptible to osteoporosis in later life. Osteoporosis is a condition related to aging in which bones lose their strength and become more likely to break. For teens who entered puberty later than most of their peers and are now reaching young adulthood, it is important to start and maintain eating and exercise habits, such as load-bearing exercises, that will strengthen bones.

As puberty comes to an end, many possibilities open up for teens.

more adult responsibilities and make their way in the world. Puberty, with its physical changes and emotional ups and downs, subsides, and teens are ready to become the adults they want to be. The future is filled with possibilities.

FACTS ABOUT PUBERTY

- Puberty marks the transition from childhood to adulthood.

- Puberty typically occurs during the preteen and teenage years.

- Changes that occur during puberty include physical growth and sexual maturation, including the ability to reproduce. There are also emotional and cognitive changes.

IMPACT ON DAILY LIFE

- Puberty brings physical changes that can take getting used to, as well as the need to develop coping skills for dealing with those changes.

- When teens go through puberty, their relationships change, making friends as important or more important than family. Romantic and sexual relationships may also develop.

DEALING WITH PUBERTY

- The best way to handle the challenges of puberty is to be knowledgeable about what is going to happen throughout the process. That way, teens can be prepared for what is going to happen to their bodies and emotions.

- The experiences of puberty will be easier to deal with when teens can communicate with parents, friends, and other trusted adults about what they are going through and whether they are normal.

- Because the teenage brain has not developed enough during puberty to be able to assess risky behaviors, it is important to minimize risk-taking and impulsiveness by clearly thinking through consequences before acting.

QUOTE

"There's nothing one can do to start puberty—
it just naturally begins."

—*Dr. Michael McKenna, pediatrician*

cognitive

Related to the act or process of thinking, reasoning, remembering, imagining, or learning.

defiance

A daring or bold resistance to an authority or an opposing force.

emission

The production and discharge of something.

fluctuation

A shift in the levels or amounts of something.

hygiene

Practices that create cleanliness and also maintain health and prevent disease.

hypothetical

Supposed or based on a theory rather than a reality.

menstruation

The process by which the uterus sheds its lining and discharges blood each month.

pediatrician

A doctor who specializes in care for children.

peripheral

Something that is situated away from the center of something, or on an edge.

radiation treatment

A type of cancer treatment that uses beams of intense energy to kill cancer cells.

vocal cords

Folds of tissue found in the human throat that produce the voice.

ADDITIONAL RESOURCES

SELECTED BIBLIOGRAPHY

Dunn, Kayla. "How Do Hormones Work?" *PBS Frontline*, n.d., pbs.org. Accessed 16 Apr. 2020.

Pickhardt, Carl E. "Helping Your Adolescent Manage Increased Emotional Intensity." *Psychology Today*, 2 May 2016, psychologytoday.com. Accessed 16 Apr. 2020.

"Teenagers (15–17 Years of Age)." *US Centers for Disease Control and Prevention*, 6 Mar. 2020, cdc.gov. Accessed 16 Apr. 2020.

FURTHER READINGS

Bailey, Jacqui. *Sex, Puberty, and All That Stuff: A Guide to Growing Up*. B.E.S., 2016.

Burling, Alexis. *Body Image and Dysmorphia*. Abdo, 2022.

Ford, Jeanne Marie. *Understanding Reproductive Health*. Abdo, 2021.

ONLINE RESOURCES

To learn more about puberty, please visit **abdobooklinks.com** or scan this QR code. These links are routinely monitored and updated to provide the most current information available.

MORE INFORMATION

For more information on this subject, contact or visit the following organizations:

Planned Parenthood Federation of America

123 William St., Tenth Floor
New York, NY 10038
plannedparenthood.org

Planned Parenthood provides reproductive health services and education, promotes research into reproductive health care, and advocates for universal access to reproductive care.

Teen Line

Cedars-Sinai Medical Center
P.O. Box 48750
Los Angeles, CA 90048
teenlineonline.org

Teen Line is a nonprofit organization that helps teens deal with their problems with the help of other teens through a national hotline, text and chat services, and community outreach.

SOURCE NOTES

CHAPTER 1. WHAT'S GOING ON?

1. Rob Haskell. "How Billie Eilish Is Reinventing Pop Stardom." *Vogue*, 3 Feb. 2020, vogue.com. Accessed 29 July 2020.
2. Robin Nixon. "Adolescent Angst: 5 Facts about the Teen Brain." *LiveScience*, 9 July 2012, livescience.com. Accessed 29 July 2020.
3. Maria Pasquini. "Emma Roberts Talks Body Image: 'I Used to Have a Complex about Being Short.'" *People*, 9 Nov. 2017, people.com. Accessed 29 July 2020.

CHAPTER 2. REPRODUCTIVE AND ENDOCRINE SYSTEMS

1. Jennifer Knudtson and Jessica E. McLaughlin. "Female External Genital Organs." *Merck Manuals*, Apr. 2019, merckmanuals.com. Accessed 29 July 2020.
2. SUNY Downstate Medical Center. "Scientists Find Hormone Activity Explains Adolescent Mood Swings." *ScienceDaily*, 12 Mar. 2007, sciencedaily.com. Accessed 29 July 2020.
3. "What Is Intersex?" *Intersex Society of North America*, n.d., isna.org. Accessed 29 July 2020.
4. Hans Lindahl. "9 Young People on How They Found Out They Are Intersex." *Teen Vogue*, 25 Oct. 2019, teenvogue.com. Accessed 29 July 2020.
5. Sarah Spinks. "Inside the Teenage Brain." *Frontline*, 31 Jan. 2002, pbs.org. Accessed 29 July 2020.

CHAPTER 3. AGES AND STAGES

1. Rena Goldman. "The Stages of Puberty: Development in Girls and Boys." *Healthline*, 23 Aug. 2018, healthline.com. Accessed 29 July 2020.
2. "Children, Youth, Families and Socioeconomic Status." *American Psychological Association*, 2010, apa.org. Accessed 29 July 2020.
3. "What Pediatricians Want You to Know about Puberty." *Riley Children's Health*, 29 Mar. 2016, rileychildrens.org. Accessed 29 July 2020.
4. Goldman, "The Stages of Puberty."
5. Tara Fowler. "Rae Carson Talks the 'Fire and Thorns' Trilogy." *Entertainment Weekly*, 13 Sept. 2012, ew.com. Accessed 29 July 2020.

CHAPTER 4. BEING PREPARED

1. Ellen Sturm Niz. "9 Ways to Prepare Your Daughter for Her First Period." *Parents*, n.d., parents.com. Accessed 29 July 2020.
2. Sturm Niz, "9 Ways to Prepare Your Daughter for Her First Period."
3. Sturm Niz, "9 Ways to Prepare Your Daughter for Her First Period."
4. "Emily Ratajkowski Penned an Essay for 'Harper's Bazaar' on Femininity, Body Hair, and Double Standards." *Teen Vogue*, 8 Aug. 2019, teenvogue.com. Accessed 29 July 2020.
5. Macaela Mackenzie. "Why You Definitely Shouldn't Pick at That Pimple, According to Dermatologists." *Allure*, 13 June 2017, allure.com. Accessed 29 July 2020.
6. Alyssa Hardy. "Teen Shares Viral Acne Message on Instagram." *Teen Vogue*, 4 Jan. 2018, teenvogue.com. Accessed 30 July 2020.

CHAPTER 5. MENTAL AND EMOTIONAL CHANGES

1. Brooke Hauser. "Drew Barrymore: Her *Allure* Photo Shoot." *Allure*, 18 Dec. 2012, allure.com. Accessed 29 July 2020.
2. Frances E. Jensen and Amy Ellis Nutt. *The Teenage Brain*. HarperCollins, 2015. 80.
3. "The Teen Brain: 7 Things to Know." *National Institute of Mental Health*, 2020, nimh.nih.gov. Accessed 29 July 2020.
4. Lindsay Piercy. "What a New Study Reveals about Selfies and Teenage Body Image." *Phys.org*, 30 May 2018, phys.org. Accessed 29 July 2020.
5. Carl E. Pickhardt. "Adolescence and the Influence of Parents." *Psychology Today*, 20 Sept. 2010, psychologytoday.com. Accessed 29 July 2020.
6. "Puberty." *Let's Talk Teens, Sexuality & Media*, n.d., depts.washington.edu. Accessed 29 July 2020.
7. "Justin Bieber Reveals First Crush." *US Weekly*, 13 Feb. 2010, usmagazine.com. Accessed 29 July 2020.
8. Gladys Martinez et al. "Educating Teenagers about Sex in the United States." *Centers for Disease Control and Prevention*, Sept. 2010, cdc.gov. Accessed 29 July 2020.

CHAPTER 6. TOO EARLY? TOO LATE?

1. "Precocious Puberty." *National Organization for Rare Disorders*, 2016, rarediseases.org. Accessed 29 July 2020.

2. Julia Corcoran. "He Started Puberty When He Was 2 Years Old. Now, He's Sharing His Experience." *WAMU*, 29 Jan. 2019, wamu.org. Accessed 29 July 2020.

3. "Precocious Puberty." *Mayo Clinic*, n.d., mayoclinic.org. Accessed 29 July 2020.

4. "McCune-Albright Syndrome." *Genetic and Rare Diseases Information Center*, 2020, rarediseases.info.nih.gov. Accessed 29 July 2020.

5. "About Neurofibromatosis." *National Human Genome Research Institute*, 16 Aug. 2016, genome.gov. Accessed 29 July 2020.

6. Kirsten Weir. "The Risks of Earlier Puberty." *American Psychological Association*, Mar. 2016, apa.org. Accessed 29 July 2020.

7. Weir, "The Risks of Earlier Puberty."

8. "Endocrine Disruptors." *National Institute of Environmental Health Sciences*, 28 July 2020, niehs.nih.gov. Accessed 29 July 2020.

9. Michelle Roberts. "Faulty 'Delayed Puberty' Gene Found." *BBC News*, 25 Mar. 2014, bbc.com. Accessed 29 July 2020.

10. Lisa Rapaport. "Puberty Timing Influenced by Both Parents." *Reuters*, 15 Apr. 2016, reuters.com. Accessed 29 July 2020.

CHAPTER 7. HANDLING THE CHANGES

1. Mary L. Gavin. "Learning about Calories." *KidsHealth*, June 2018, kidshealth.org. Accessed 29 July 2020.

2. Office of Adolescent Health. "April 2018: Eating Disorders in Adolescence." *Office of Population Affairs*, 18 Apr. 2018, hhs.gov. Accessed 29 July 2020.

3. Jessica Bruso. "When Does a Teen's Metabolism Slow Down?" *Livestrong*, n.d., livestrong.com. Accessed 29 July 2020.

4. Brittney McNamara. "Research Looks at Why Puberty Happens in Teen Years." *Teen Vogue*, 3 Jan. 2019, teenvogue.com. Accessed 29 July 2020.

5. Carl E. Pickhardt. "Adolescence and the Importance of Talking to Parents." *Psychology Today*, 12 Nov. 2018, psychologytoday.com. Accessed 29 July 2020.

6. *Stress in America: Generation Z*. American Psychological Association, October 2018. 2–4.

CHAPTER 8. RELATIONSHIPS AND PUBERTY

1. "Abusive Relationships." *Planned Parenthood*, n.d., plannedparenthood.org. Accessed 29 July 2020.

2. Monica Anderson and Jinging Jiang. "Teens' Social Media Habits and Experiences." *Pew Research Center*, 28 Nov. 2019, pewresearch.org. Accessed 29 July 2020.

3. "Social Media and Teens." *American Academy of Child & Adolescent Psychiatry*, Mar. 2018, aacap.org. Accessed 29 July 2020.

4. "Child Welfare." *Youth.gov*, n.d., youth.gov. Accessed 29 July 2020.

5. Serena Sonoma. "What Dating and Love Is Like for Nonbinary People." *Teen Vogue*, 14 Feb. 2019, teenvogue.com. Accessed 29 July 2020.

CHAPTER 9. THE FUTURE BEGINS

1. Anna Klepchukova. "When Does Puberty End for Girls? Flo's Puberty Guide." *Flo*, 14 Apr. 2020, flo.health. Accessed 29 July 2020.

2. "Our Culture." *Mescalero Apache Tribe*, n.d., mescaleroapachetribe.com. Accessed 29 July 2020.

3. Rachel Moss. "Medieval Millennials." *History Today*, 4 June 2018, historytoday.com. Accessed 29 July 2020.

4. Agence France-Presse. "Going through Puberty on Screen Was Terrifying: 23-Year-Old Oscar Veteran, Soairse Ronan." *Hindustan Times*, 20 Feb. 2018, hindustantimes.com. Accessed 29 July 2020.

5. "Early and Middle Adulthood." *Lumen Learning*, n.d., courses.lumenlearning.com. Accessed 29 July 2020.

MARCIA AMIDON LUSTED

Marcia Amidon Lusted has written 175 books and more than 600 magazine articles for young readers. She is also an editor and works in the field of sustainable development.

ABOUT THE CONSULTANT

CYNTHIA CORBITT

Cynthia Corbitt, PhD, is an associate professor of biology at the University of Louisville, where she teaches Endocrinology and Behavioral Endocrinology, among other courses.

Dr. Corbitt's research focus is environmental signaling, meaning factors originating outside of our bodies (diet, pesticides, cigarette smoke, social interactions) that affect the function of our bodies, especially our endocrine and nervous systems. Dr. Corbitt actively participates in public outreach for science education via the March for Science, the Society for Neuroscience, and Brain Awareness Week.